# WHAT IF THE SHARK WEARS TENNIS SHOES!

Atheneum
Macmillan Publishing Company
866 Third Avenue, New York, NY 10022
Collier Macmillan Canada, Inc.
First Edition
Printed in Hong Kong

10  9  8  7  6  5  4  3  2  1

Library of Congress Cataloging-in-Publication Data
Morris, Winifred.
What if the shark wears tennis shoes?/by Winifred Morris;
illustrated by Betsy Lewin.   p.   cm.
Summary: Stephen's nighttime fear materializes—a shark that gets
all the way upstairs and into his room to try to eat him—but
Stephen has an alternative suggestion.
ISBN 0-689-31587-2
[1. Sharks—Fiction.   2. Fear—Fiction.   3. Bedtime—Fiction.]
I. Lewin, Betsy, ill.   II. Title.
PZ7.M82923Wh   1990   [E]—dc20
89-38150   CIP   AC

# WHAT IF THE SHARK WEARS TENNIS SHOES?

*by Winifred Morris / illustrated by Betsy Lewin*

**Atheneum    1990    New York**

For Susan Allen, just the right neighbor at just the right time.
—W. M.

To my brother, John
—B. L.

Stephen brushed his teeth and put on his pajamas, but he didn't crawl into bed.

Instead, he sat in the middle of his bed and held his knees tight under his chin.

When his mother came upstairs to kiss him good night, he said, "Stay with me. I'm too scared to sleep."

"But there's nothing to be afraid of," his mother assured him. "Nothing can hurt you here in your bed."

Stephen wasn't so sure. He said, "What if a shark comes? What if he eats me?"

"That's impossible," said his mother. "Sharks live in the ocean."

"You don't know everything," Stephen told her. "What if just one shark got tired of living in the ocean? And what if he's going to come here tonight?"

"You ask too many questions. Where do you get such silly ideas? We live too far from the ocean for a shark to be able to get here."

Stephen wasn't so sure.

"Now, good night," said his mother.

"But," said Stephen, "what if he hitchhikes? I bet a shark would like to hitchhike. I bet a big, hungry shark would like to get a ride in a station wagon full of boys like me."

"No one would give him a ride," said his mother.

"Then what if he steals a Ferrari? I bet a shark would like to steal a Ferrari and offer rides to boys like me."

"You ask too many questions. Where do you get such silly ideas? A shark couldn't find you here in your house."

Stephen wasn't so sure.

"Now, good night," said his mother.

"No!" said Stephen. "What if he has a compass and a map? What if he learned how to use them at camp? I bet at his camp he would also learn how to follow the tracks left by boys like me."

"We always lock our house at night."

"What if he has a key?" asked Stephen. "What if he always carries lots of spare keys, because he uses them like files to sharpen his teeth?"
"He couldn't climb the stairs to your room," said his mother.
Stephen wasn't so sure.

"What if he uses a pick and a rope? I bet that would work. I'm sure it would. Couldn't he haul himself up the stairs with a pick and a rope?"

"That would make a lot of noise. You would hear him," said his mother. "And I would hear him. And your father would hear him."

"But what if you don't?" asked Stephen. "What if the shark wears tennis shoes? Then he'd be really quiet. He'd come into my room. And then…"

Stephen shuddered. He held his knees tighter. He stared wide-eyed at the head of the stairs.

His mother shook her head. "I don't know where you get these silly ideas. And I don't have time for all these questions. Now good night. Sleep tight." She turned off the light.

And before Stephen could say any more, she had left. So he had to wait there all by himself—until the shark came.

Quickly he hid under the covers. From there, even
though it was dark, he could see the shark throw his pick
up the stairs. Then the shark hauled himself to the top
with a rope. When the shark pulled the rope up behind
him, Stephen saw a huge bowl attached to it. Next came
a big jug of milk—and last, a bag of sugar.

Stephen was trying to be as quiet as a pillow. But by the time the shark had pulled the sugar up the stairs, he just had to ask one question.

He said, "What are you going to do with all of that?"

"What do you think?" snarled the shark, now looking right at Stephen. "You think boys are tender? You think boys are sweet? The only way I can choke them down is with lots of milk and sugar."

The shark had huge teeth and tiny, mean eyes. But from under the covers, Stephen managed to say, "Then why do you eat them?"

"You ask too many questions. Just get into the bowl. Let's get this over with."

"But what if you tried eating cereal instead? I bet a shark might like cereal. With all that milk and sugar, I bet a big, hungry shark would like cereal even better than boys like me."

"Cereal? What's cereal?" said the shark.

"Promise not to eat me if I show you?"

"Mmmmm," the shark sighed, slurping cereal through
his pointed teeth. "Where do you get such great ideas?"

The next morning, when Stephen's mother came into the kitchen, she said, "No one could make this much mess!"

"You don't know everything," Stephen told her. "What if a shark was here last night? What if he ate up all the cereal? I bet a shark would like to make this much mess."